LET'S GET ALONG!

It's Great to Keep Calm

Jordan Collins • Stuart Lynch

make believe ideas

"Good morning, class!" said Miss Clayton.

"We're having a sock puppet show today!"

The class cheered.

They'd never had a sock puppet show before!

"And," Miss Clayton added,
"you'll be making your own sock puppets."
The class cheered again.

Carly **couldn't wait** to get started.

She **loved** making art, and her parents said she was **good at it.**

Carly felt certain she was going to make the
best sock puppet in the class.

Carly **rushed** to the table of art supplies.
She took everything – **except** the sheet that showed
how to put the puppet together.

Carly had never made a sock puppet before,
but she was **sure** she didn't need pictures like everyone else.

After a few minutes, Carly noticed that her puppet's nose **wouldn't stay on.**

She had to add **more and more** glue.

Then the glue **leaked** through the sock and got all over her hands.

Carly **frowned** and started over again.

"Good work, class!" called out Miss Clayton.

"That puppet looks great, Emily!" she added.

Everybody admired Emily's sock puppet –

except Carly.

glue

Why doesn't **mine**

look like that? Carly thought.

Carly **yanked** a felt eye off her puppet.

It was a mess: there was **gooey glue** all over the puppet's face, and when she tried to make it talk, the sock stuck to her fingers.

"Yuck!" she said to herself.

Carly started to feel **upset**.

Her palms were **sweaty**, and her heart was **beating fast**.

Everybody else had **already finished** their sock puppets.

Not only that, their puppets looked like they belonged in a show.

Carly's looked like a **soggy, sticky** disaster.
She couldn't understand why her puppet had gone **so wrong**.

"Do you want help?" Jack asked.

"No!" Carly yelled in frustration. "I can do it by myself."

She was upset with **everybody**, especially **herself**.

It just wasn't fair!

Carly tried to pull off the sock
so she could start over,
but she **pulled too hard**.

It landed in a
wet heap on the floor.

Carly stomped on it.

"I don't want to make a sock puppet anyway," she said.

But Carly **did** want to make a sock puppet.

Her eyes filled with **hot tears**, and she squeezed her hands into **fists**.

"Are you okay?" Jack asked.

"I feel like I'm getting **everything wrong** today," Carly said.

Her shoulders shook, and she began to cry.

"My mom says that if I get upset, I should take deep breaths and give myself **a hug**," Jack said.

Carly tried it:
she took some **deep breaths**
and gave herself **a hug**.

After a few seconds,
she didn't want to cry so much
and she began to **relax**.

"I'm sorry I yelled at you," Carly told Jack.

"If you're feeling better, I can help you," Jack said.

"Even though I yelled?" Carly asked.

"It hurt my feelings," Jack said, "but you're still my friend. Everyone loses their temper sometimes." "Thanks," Carly said.

The friends picked up more supplies,
and this time Carly grabbed an instruction sheet.

With Jack's help,
she made a sock puppet
with a proper nose,
eyes, and tongue, all in the
right places.

It looked great!

Carly hugged Jack.

"Thanks for helping me calm down," she said.

"Now I've got a sock puppet, too!"

It was almost time for the show. Carly and Jack went to the stage.
"Ready?" asked Jack. "Ready!" said Carly.

READING TOGETHER

The **Let's Get Along!** books have been written for parents, caregivers, and teachers to share with young children who are developing an awareness of their own behavior.

The books are intended to initiate thinking around behavior and empower children to create positive circumstances by managing their actions. Each book can be used to gently promote further discussion around the topic featured.

It's Great to Stay Calm is designed to help children realize that when things don't go as expected and they feel anxious or angry, there are actions they can take to calm down. Once you have read the story together, go back and talk about any similar experiences the children might have had with feeling upset (and also with calming down). Explain that while trusted adults and friends can often help, there are times when children can also help themselves. Ensure that children understand that everyone gets anxious or loses their temper sometimes and that, like Carly, they can take steps to calm down and try again.

As you read

By asking children questions as you read together, you can help them engage more deeply with the story. While it is important not to ask too many questions, you can try a few simple questions, such as:

- What do you think will happen next?

- Why do you think Carly did that?

- What would you do if you were Carly?

- How does Carly calm herself?

Look at the pictures

Talk about the pictures. Is Carly smiling, laughing, frowning, or confused? Does her body position show how she is feeling? Discuss why she might be responding this way. As children build their awareness of how others are feeling, they will find it easier to respond with understanding.

Questions you can ask after reading

To prompt further exploration of this behavior, you could ask children some of the following questions:

- What things could you do to calm yourself down? Would you hug yourself, take deep breaths, walk away, get some fresh air, or something else?

- How can you tell if someone else is upset and struggling to calm down?

- How can you help someone who is upset?

- It is good to be able to calm yourself, but sometimes you should talk to a trusted grown-up as well. Can you think of any times when this would be a good idea?